Better Homes and Gardens®

LET'S PRETEND

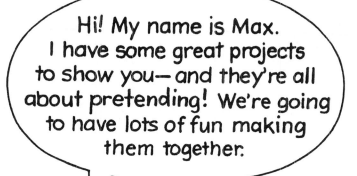

Hi! My name is Max. I have some great projects to show you—and they're all about pretending! We're going to have lots of fun making them together.

© Copyright 1988 by Meredith Corporation, Des Moines, Iowa.
All Rights Reserved. Printed in the United States of America.
First Edition. Third Printing, 1989.
ISBN: 0-696-01900-0 (hard cover)
ISBN: 0-696-01813-6 (trade paperback)
MAX THE DRAGON™ and other characters in this book are trademarks and copyrighted
characters of Meredith Corporation, and their use by others is strictly prohibited.

Inside You'll Find...

Pretend You're an Explorer

Max and his best friend, Elliot, are on an exciting adventure in a faraway land. This jungle is filled with all sorts of wild animals. Which one is your favorite?

4

Find the Monkeys?

Look! There are 6 monkeys watching Max and Elliot. Can you point to them?

When you go exploring, do you ever get hungry? Max does, too. Here's his favorite snack—it's really easy to fix!

Jungle Mix

- In a paper sack or a large plastic bag, combine 2 cups dried banana chips; 1 cup corn bran cereal, toasted oat cereal, or bran squares cereal; 1 cup peanuts or whole almonds; and ½ cup pumpkin or sunflower seed.
- Close bag and shake well.
- Eat right away or store in the bag up to 1 month.
- Makes about 4 cups.

A homemade camera fit for an at-home safari.

Box Camera

Be sure to take a camera with you when you go exploring. Snap pictures of wild animals, rivers and mountains, or anything else you might see. This camera works great on a safari.

What you'll need...

- 1 small cereal, pudding, or gelatin box
- Aluminum foil
- Tape
- Crafts knife
- 1 large cork
- 1 piece of yarn, about 28 inches long

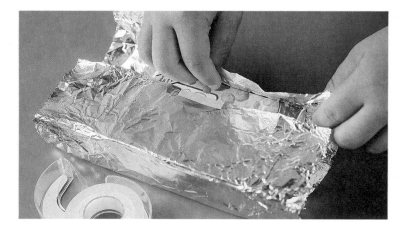

1 Wrap the box with foil like a present (see photo). Tape ends. For the viewfinder, with adult help, use a crafts knife to cut a small square in upper right-hand corner, about ¼ inch from edges. Turn box over and cut another square, opposite the first square.

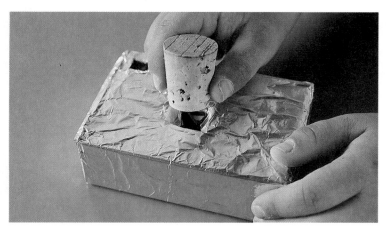

2 For the lens, with adult help, use the crafts knife to cut an X the size of the large cork in the center of the box. Push in cut edges. Insert the large cork into the opening (see photo).

3 For the strap, tape the ends of the yarn to the sides of the camera.

The perfect craft for young explorers to make.

Safari Binoculars

Don't forget to take your binoculars! You'll need them when searching for lost cities of gold or a herd of wild elephants.

What you'll need...

- Two 4½-inch cardboard tubes (toilet paper tubes)
- Colored cellophane, cut into 3-inch circles
- Tape
- Construction paper, cut into two 4½x6-inch pieces
- Pencil
- Yarn, cut into two 24-inch pieces

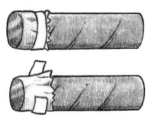

1 Cover one end of each tube with cellophane. Tape cellophane to tube.

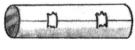
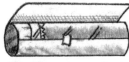

2 Cover each tube with a piece of construction paper. Tape paper to tubes. Place tubes side by side. Tape tubes together.

With a pencil, poke a hole in outside edges of tubes about ½ inch from ends. Use pencil to poke one end of yarn through each hole. Tie each end to prevent it from slipping out.

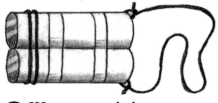

3 Wrap remaining yarn around other ends of tubes to cover tape; tie.

What Do You See?

One pleasant, warm day, Max was playing in his backyard.
When he looked up at the sky, he saw a big cloud.
It looked like a smiling whale. Look at the picture.
What do you see?

Max was able to find 12 things hiding in his backyard. How about you? Can you point to the car, sailboat, whale, turtles, giant caterpillar, porcupine, elephants, and lizards?

Let paint and brush spur creativity.

Pretend You're an Artist

Do you ever play make-believe? It's fun to pretend to be anyone you want to be. Make believe that you have just turned into an artist who paints beautiful pictures. What else would you make as an artist?

Imagine Things as They Might Be

Artists, writers, inventors, and musicians see and hear things in new and different ways. Close your eyes. Think of something in a different way. Imagine how it would look and sound.

Make up something, or paint one of these scenes:

● Can you imagine...a monkey in a banana tree...eating ice cream...reading a book...while a polka-dotted elephant blows a horn?

● Can you imagine...a giant orange shark...wearing a yellow mask and cape...riding a green bicycle...while pulling a pink cow in a wagon?

Oatmeal cookies become family portraits.

Funny-Face Cookies

Make these big cookies look like your Dad and Mom or your Grandpa and Grandma, or even you. And the best part is—these picture cookies are good enough to eat!

What you'll need...

- Narrow metal spatula or table knife
- Peanut butter or canned chocolate frosting
- Funny-Face Cookies (see page 31) or purchased cookies
- Cookie decorations (see opposite)

1 Using a narrow metal spatula, "paint" the top of each cookie with peanut butter.

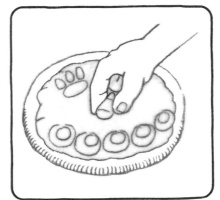

2 "Draw" faces of people on the cookies with cookie decorations.

Pretend You're a Pizza Chef

Max likes to make-believe he owns a pizza restaurant. Do you like to eat pizza? Max's favorite kind is pepperoni with lots of mushrooms. What's yours?

MEDIUM
5¢

LARGE
10¢

SMALL
1¢

Pennies and Pizza Slices

Max is selling three different sizes of pizza slices. Can you point to the small, the medium, and the large pizza slices? Look at the pizza signs... How much does a small slice cost? Answer: 1¢.

How much does a medium slice cost? Answer: 5¢.

How much does a large slice cost? Answer: 10¢.

Every make-believe world needs a hat to match.

Paper Hat

Max wears his hat when he sells pizza or when he's a doctor, pilot, forest ranger, or police officer. What do you want to be when you wear your hat?

What you'll need...

● One 20-inch by 2½-ft. piece of white gift wrap or shelf paper

1 Fold paper in half crosswise. Crease all folds well. Place fold at top (as shown).

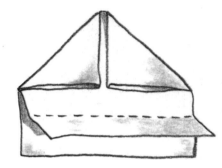

2 Fold upper corners to meet in center. Fold up top piece to meet two upper folds.

3 Fold the top piece up again to cover bottom of upper folds.

4 Turn hat over. Fold left side in to center (as shown).

5 Repeat with right side. (For larger hat, don't fold sides all the way in to center.)

6 Fold up the bottom edge twice to cover upper folds, as with top piece (see Steps 2 and 3).

7 Tuck flap into the "hat band." Fold down the point and tuck it into the hat band.

Make-Believe Hats

Hats are fun to wear. Did you know that sometimes people wear special hats while they work or play? What's your favorite hat?

Put on your "thinking cap" and guess what Max and his friends are pretending to be.

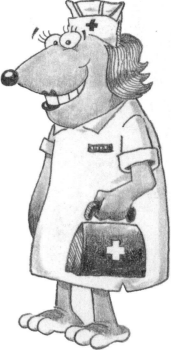

Pretend You're a Mail Carrier

Did you know that mail carriers bring catalogs, packages, and letters to your house? Max is ready to deliver mail to his friends. Can you help him find the right mailboxes?

This is a seed catalog. You can order vegetable and flower seeds from it. What path should Max take to deliver this catalog?

This package has a birthday present wrapped up inside. Look at the pictures and decide who gets the package.

This is a letter. Someone is playing outside while waiting for Max to deliver the mail. Which one of Max's friends gets the letter?

18

A paper-sack mailbag that holds letters.

Lick 'n' Stick Stamps

What does Max lick and then stick on a letter, a postcard, or a package before he mails it? It's called a postage stamp. Here's how you can make your own stamps.

What you'll need...

- Scissors
- 1½-inch-wide packaging tape (the kind you moisten)
- Envelopes
- Crayons or markers

1 For each stamp, cut off a piece of the packaging tape about 1½ inches long.

2 Lick the stamps and stick them to the envelopes.

3 Color the stamps. If you like, put numbers on the stamps to show how much they cost.

A supermarket paper sack becomes a mailbag.

Paper-Sack Mailbag

To be a mail carrier and deliver all the mail to your family and friends, you'll need a big mailbag. How about making this one?

What you'll need...

- 1 large paper sack
- Masking tape
- Crayons or markers
- Stapler

- 1 strip of cloth or piece of yarn, about 24 inches long

1 Fold down the top edge of the paper sack about 3 inches. Be sure to fold the edge toward the inside of the sack. Tape the edge to the inside of the sack.

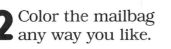

2 Color the mailbag any way you like.

3 For the shoulder strap, tape or staple the ends of the cloth to the inside of the sack.

Pretend You're a Musician

Max and his friends are musicians in a band. They enjoy playing their instruments and making music. Can you name the musical instruments in Max's band?

Let's listen to Max's band. Hoot 'n' toot goes the horn.

Rat-a-tat-tat goes the drum.

Clang and bang go the cymbals.

Let's give them a big hand. They're the best in the land!

22

Making Music

Take a look at these objects. Some of them do not belong in a band. Can you point to the ones that will make a musical sound? Can you name the instruments that you would like to play in your band?

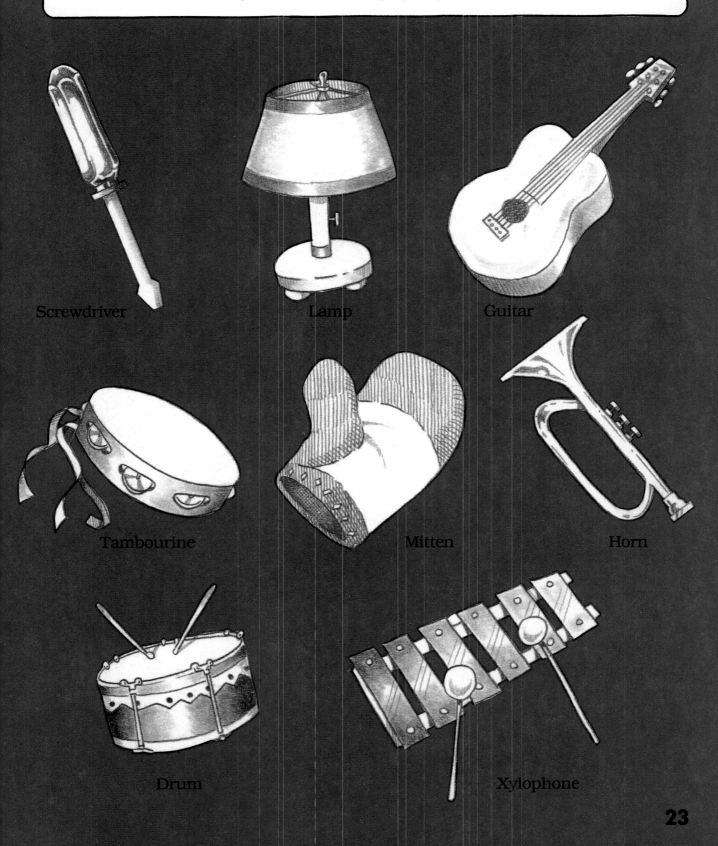

Screwdriver

Lamp

Guitar

Tambourine

Mitten

Horn

Drum

Xylophone

Make musical instruments from household items.

Music Makers

You don't need fancy instruments to make music. It's easy to make the Sandpaper Blocks and Hummer Horn.

Sandpaper Blocks
What you'll need...

- One 4x9-inch piece fine sandpaper, torn in half
- 2 small cereal, pudding, or gelatin boxes
- Masking tape

Hummer Horn
What you'll need...

- Waxed paper, cut into 4½-inch square
- 1 paper towel tube
- 1 rubber band
- Pencil

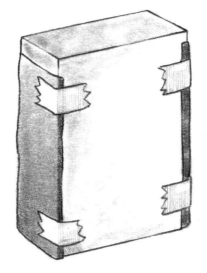

1 For each Sandpaper Block, wrap 1 piece of sandpaper around 1 box. The sandpaper will not go all the way around the box.

2 Fasten sandpaper to the box with masking tape. Repeat with remaining box and paper.
   To play, rub the sandpaper sides together.

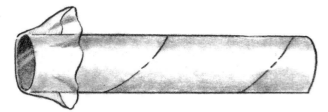

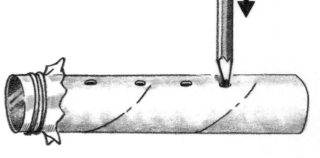

1 For the Hummer Horn, place the waxed paper over one end of the paper towel tube. Fasten the waxed paper to the tube with a rubber band.

2 With a pencil, poke holes in the tube for finger holes.
   To play, put your mouth next to the open end of the tube. Hum into the tube while you cover and uncover the finger holes.

Max and his friends enjoy pretending that they're in a marching band. How about you? Can you march and play your instrument?

Decorate an empty oatmeal box to make a drum.

Rap-and-Tap Drum

Boom! Boom! Boom! Rump-a-pum-pum! These are the wonderful musical sounds you can make by playing your drum.

What you'll need...

- 1 round oatmeal box (18-ounce)
- One 7x12-inch piece construction paper
- Tape
- One 24-inch piece of yarn
- Crayons or markers
- Pencil
- 4 cotton balls
- 2 unsharpened pencils
- Plastic wrap, cut into two 6-inch circles
- 2 rubber bands

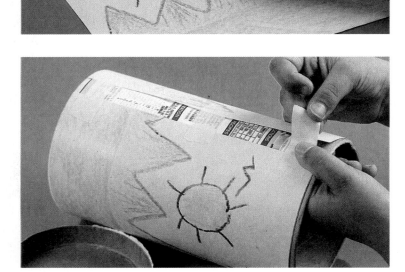

1 For the Rap-and-Tap Drum, remove the lid from the oatmeal box. Color the piece of construction paper any way you like. Cover the outside of the container with the construction paper (it will not cover box completely). Fasten with tape.

2 With a pencil, poke two holes opposite each other about 1 inch from the top edge of the box. Use the pencil to poke one end of the yarn through each hole. Tie each end of the yarn inside the box to prevent it from slipping out of the holes. Replace the lid.

3 For each drumstick, wrap 2 cotton balls around the unsharpened end of a pencil. Wrap the plastic-wrap circle over the cotton. Secure with a rubber band.

Make a Drum

The drum is one of the easiest—and most fun—musical instruments you can make. Take a look at the drums in the picture below for some ideas.

Painting an empty oatmeal box with tempera paints makes a beautiful drum, too. If you have some pretty feathers, glue them to the drum.

Animal antics for kids to act out.

Pretend You're a Frog

Imagine that you're a big green frog. How high can you jump? Make believe that you could change yourself into any animal you wanted. What would it be? How would you . . .

Leap like a frog?

Waddle like a penguin?

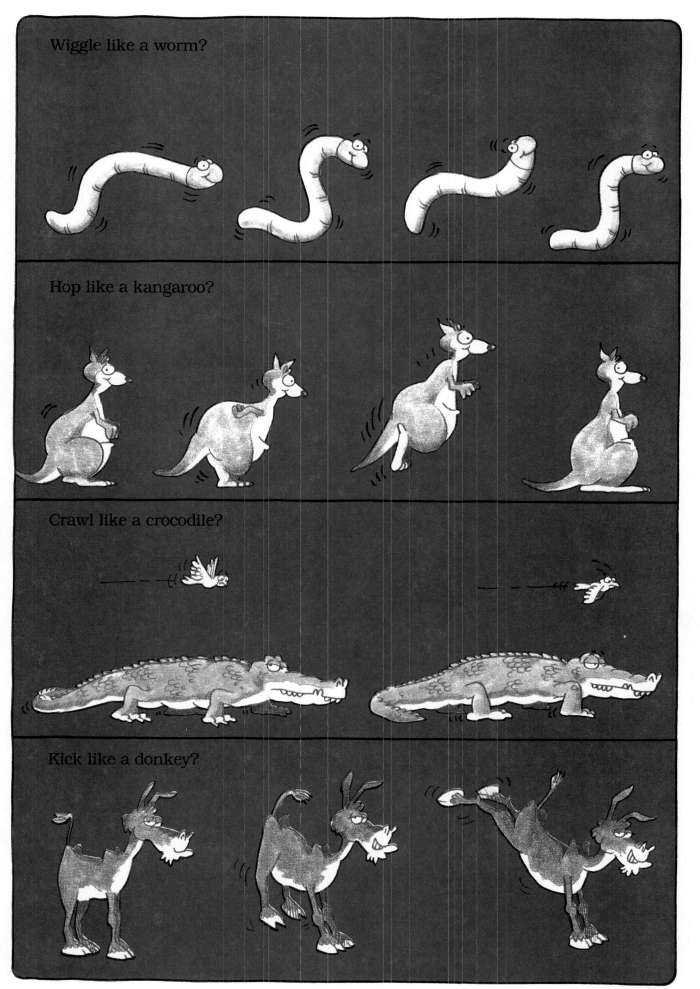

Wiggle like a worm?

Hop like a kangaroo?

Crawl like a crocodile?

Kick like a donkey?

Parents' Pages

We've filled this special section with more activities, recipes, reading suggestions, hints we learned from our kid-testers, and many more helpful tips.

Pretend You're An Explorer

See pages 4 and 5

Children are natural explorers! Ask your children if they could be explorers anywhere in the world...
- Where would they go?
- How would they get there?
- What would they find?
- How long would they stay?
Have them tell you about it.

Here's a fun project for young explorers. Gather rocks and let your children paint them all different colors. Put each rock in an empty egg carton cup. Let the rocks dry. Without your children knowing it, hide the rocks somewhere in your house or backyard. Then let your children look for the "hidden treasures." You can give them clues or draw a map of where the rocks are hidden.

Box Camera And Safari Binoculars

See pages 6 and 7

Tell your children a safari is an adventurous trip or a hunting expedition taken by a group of people. Then ask them what they would take with them on their safari. A camera and binoculars are just a start. Maybe your children would take a map, a hat, or a flashlight. If a backpack is available, let them fill it with all their safari gear.

What Do You See?

See pages 8 and 9

A delightful activity to share with your children is to look at the sky when it's full of huge, puffy white clouds. Ask them, "What does that cloud look like to you?" Soon they'll be seeing imaginary things.
- Reading suggestions:
The Trek by Ann Jonas
Dreams by Peter Spier

Pretend You're An Artist

See pages 10 and 11

Painting allows young children to experiment. Their free-style pictures help them practice line pressure and various forms (straight or zigzag lines, circles, squares).

Every picture doesn't have to "look like something."
- Reading suggestion:
An Artist by M. B. Goffstein

Fun Painting Materials

Let your children paint with water colors, tempera paints, and fingerpaints. But don't stop there. Let them experiment with other "paints."

Paint with Chocolate Pudding
Cover the work surface with newspapers. Give your children a piece of fingerpaint paper, waxed paper, or shelf paper. Let them spread out a large spoonful of pudding or chocolate syrup mixed with a little water on their paper. The kids will love smearing it around and licking their fingers.

Paint with Shaving Cream
Dampen a waterproof surface. Spray the shaving cream on the wet surface. Then let your children paint with their fingers and hands. A wet sponge is all it takes to wash their little hands and the surface.

Funny-Face Cookies

See pages 12 and 13

Encourage your children's creative self-expression by helping them decorate cookies. Here's our recipe for homemade oatmeal cookies.

Funny-Face Cookies

- 1 cup all-purpose flour
- 1 cup whole wheat flour
- ½ teaspoon baking soda
- ½ cup margarine or butter
- ½ cup shortening
- ⅔ cup sugar
- ⅔ cup packed brown sugar
- 2 eggs
- ¼ cup milk
- 1 teaspoon vanilla
- 2 cups quick-cooking rolled oats
- ½ cup chopped walnuts

● Lightly grease cookie sheet. In a small bowl stir together the flours and baking soda.
● In mixer bowl beat margarine or butter and shortening with an electric mixer for 30 seconds. Add the sugars. Beat till fluffy.
● Add eggs, milk, and vanilla and beat well. Gradually add the flour mixture, beating till combined. Stir in the rolled oats and walnuts.
● For each cookie, drop about ¼ cup of dough onto the greased cookie sheet. Spread the dough into a 3-inch circle. Space the cookies about 3 inches apart.
● Bake in a 375° oven about 12 minutes or till bottoms are lightly browned. Cool on cookie sheet for 1 minute. Remove from cookie sheet and cool completely on wire racks. Repeat with remaining dough.
● Frost and trim cooled cookies as directed on page 12. Makes about 18.

Pretend You're A Pizza Chef

See pages 14 and 15

A playful fantasy is usually irresistible to children. Help them get started by collecting some dramatic play props.

Some good items to collect and have on hand are: hats (western, hard hat, fire fighter, straw hat, scarf), stick horse, neckerchief, telephone, lunch bucket, play money, plastic fruits and vegetables, play dishes, and food cartons.

And, if you don't have something, improvise. Here's a simple and inexpensive way to make a "cash register."

Cut a cardboard egg carton in half crosswise. Turn it upside down. Use a marker to write numbers on each egg cup. Children can pretend the egg cups are cash register keys and then open the carton and put in the play money.

Paper Hat

See pages 16 and 17

Young children can be anyone they like when wearing their paper hats. Or, they can pretend to be animals.

Turn the paper hat sideways. Then cut pointed ears out of construction paper and decorate. Tape or staple them to the paper hat. Your children can pretend to be rabbits, cats, donkeys, horses, tigers, or any animal with pointed ears.

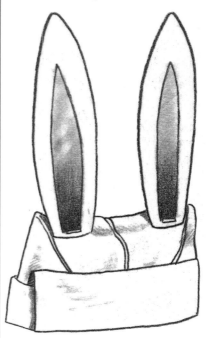

Pretend You're A Mail Carrier

See pages 18 and 19

Whether they're mail carriers, doctors, fire fighters, police officers, or airplane pilots, most preschool children enjoy having their parents join their playacting. They need you to participate and interact.

You can support their play by adding dialogue, being their audience, or extending your children's ideas. But remember not to get carried away with your own creativity and take over.

Lick 'n' Stick Stamps and Mailbag

See pages 20 and 21

Do your children show an interest in learning to write? Do they use crayons and pencils regularly for drawing? If so, help them practice writing letters to their grandparents and friends, or to you.

Give them a sheet of paper and a short, thick "primary pencil," which is easier to hold than a long, thin pencil. Encourage them to draw, scribble, and pretend to write.

Pretend You're A Musician

See pages 22 and 23

By letting your children play homemade musical instruments, sing songs and dance, and listen to the rhythmic sounds of nature, you'll help them develop their creative dramatic self-expression and promote growth in motor control. But most importantly, your children will really enjoy themselves.

Here's an activity that involves both art and music. While your children are listening to music, ask them to draw whatever they think of to match what they hear. Be sure they have a big selection of colors (crayons, markers, paints, or colored pencils).

And, vary the kind of music—from marches to ballads. They'll have a great time and you'll enjoy the way their drawings vary.

Music Makers

See pages 24 and 25

If your children like the Sandpaper Blocks and Hummer Horn, let them create other musical instruments. They can make music from just about any object. Here are some ideas:

● An empty margarine tub or sour cream container filled halfway with pebbles, dry rice, or dried beans makes music when it's shaken.

● Don't forget this old favorite—spoons. Give your children pairs of spoons and show them how to tap them against their palms.

Rap-and-Tap Drum

See pages 26 and 27

If you don't have an oatmeal box, here are some other ideas for homemade drums. An empty margarine tub, tennis ball cylinder, coffee can, and powdered drink container can become a set of drums. Each will have a different sound when your children beat on the lids.

Pretend You're A Frog

See pages 28 and 29

Young children and imaginary play are a perfect match. Playing a simple game of "Pretend You Are" helps to encourage your children's playacting. Ask them to pretend to be birds, butterflies, ducks, turtles, monkeys, bears, space creatures, monsters, dinosaurs, or anything you like.

Once you trigger their creative imaginations, the potential is boundless!

● Reading suggestions:
Where the Wild Things Are by Maurice Sendak
There's a Nightmare In My Closet by Mercer Mayer

BETTER HOMES AND GARDENS® BOOKS
Editor: Gerald M. Knox
Art Director: Ernest Shelton
Managing Editor: David Kirchner
Department Head, Food and Family Life: Sharyl Heiken

LET'S PRETEND
Editors: Sandra Granseth and Linda Foley Woodrum
Editorial Project Manager: Rosanne Weber Mattson
Graphic Designers: Linda Ford Vermie and Brian Wignall
Contributing Illustrator: Buck Jones
Contributing Photographer: Scott Little
Contributing Editor: Martha Schiel

Have BETTER HOMES AND GARDENS® magazine delivered to your door.
For information, write to:
ROBERT AUSTIN
P.O. BOX 4536
DES MOINES, IA 50336